FREE TO BE... YOU AND ME

Conceived by Marlo Thomas

Developed and Edited by Carole Hart
Letty Cottin Pogrebin, Mary Rodgers,
and Marlo Thomas

Original Editor: Francine Klagsbrun

A PROJECT OF THE MS. FOUNDATION, INC.

RP|KIDS
PHILADELPHIA • LONDON

Reynolds

Library of Congress Cataloging-in-Publication Number: 2008928610

ISBN 978-0-7624-3060-4

Acknowledgements:

Words and music for "Free to Be…You and Me," "When We Grow Up," "Sisters and Brothers," and "Helping" copyright © 1972 Ms. Foundation for Women, Inc. Used by permission.

Words and music for "Parents are People," "It's All Right to Cry," and "Glad to Have a Friend Like You," and words for "My Dog is a Plumber" copyright © 1972 Free to be Foundation, Inc.

"Atalanta" copyright © 1973 Free to Be Foundation, Inc.

"William's Doll" adapted from the book *William's Doll* by Charlotte Zolotow. Text copyright © 1972 Charlotte Zolotow. Used by permission of Harper & Row, Publishers, Inc. Words and music adaptation, copyright © 1972 Ms. Foundation for Women, Inc.

"Dudley Pippin and the Principal" by Phil Ressner, adapted from "Dudley and the Principal" from the book *Dudley Pippin* by Phil Ressner, illustrated by Arnold Lobel. Text copyright © 1965 Phil Ressner. Pictures copyright © 1965 Arnold Lobel. Reprinted by permission of Harper & Row, Publishers, Inc.

"Three Wishes" by Lucille Clifton, copyright © 1974 Lucille Clifton. Used by permission of author and Curtis Brown, Ltd.

Cover illustrated by Peter H. Reynolds, copyright © 2008.

"Free to be…You and Me," "Sisters and Brothers," "The Southpaw," "No One Else," and "Glad to Have a Friend Like You" illustrated by Peter H. Reynolds, copyright © 2008.

"Boy Meets Girl" illustrated by Joe Mathieu, copyright © 2008.

"When We Grow Up" illustrated by Lynn Munsinger, copyright © 2008.

"Don't Dress Your Cat in an Apron" illustrated by Tony diTerlizzi, copyright © 2008.

Photographs for "Parents Are People" illustrated by Henry Cole, copyright © 2008.

"Helping" illustrated by Monica Sheehan, copyright © 2008.

"The Pain and The Great One" illustrated by Jimmy Pickering, copyright © 2008.

"The Old Woman Who Lived in a Shoe" illustrated by David Catrow, copyright © 2008.

"William's Doll" illustrated by LeUyen Pham, copyright © 2008.

"My Dog is a Plumber" illustrated by Doug Taylor, copyright © 2008.

"The Field" illustrated by Jerry Pinkney, copyright © 2008.

"Three Wishes" illustrated by Christopher Myers, copyright © 2008.

"Zachary's Divorce" illustrated by Dan Andreason, copyright © 2008.

"Atalanta" illustrated by Barbara Bascove, copyright © 2008.

"If Wishes Were Fishes" written by David Slavin and illustrated by Peter Sis, copyright © 2008.

Photographs for "It's All Right to Cry" p.54: top left ©Tom Smart/Getty Images; top right ©Bigshots/Digital Vision/Getty Images; center left ©Cris Bouroncle/AFP/Getty Images; bottom left ©Joel Sartore/National Geographic/Getty Images; bottom right ©iStockphoto.com/Rob Friedman. p.55: top left ©Alex Wong/Getty Images; left, second from top ©Thomas Coex/AFP/Getty Images; top right ©Experienced Skins Vol 1/Dex Image/Getty Images; center right ©Image Source/Getty Images; bottom ©Elie Bernager/Digital Vision/Getty Images

Photographs for "Glad to Have a Friend Like You" top left © Gordon Gregory/Veer; top center ©David Young-Wolff/Photographer's Choice/Getty Images; top right ©Anne Ackermann/Taxi/Getty Images; center left ©Palomba/Veer; center right ©amana productions inc./Getty Images; bottom left ©Digital Vision Photography/Veer; bottom center ©Image Source Photography/Veer; bottom right ©Image Source/Getty Images

Photograph of Marlo Thomas by Jerry Erico.

Photograph of Marlo Thomas and friends 1972 by Kenn Duncan, furnished courtesy of Bell Records.

Piano arrangements for this book by Stephen Lawrence.

Musical score for "William's Doll" prepared and edited by Dan Sovak.

The new edition was a creative collaboration! Running Press, Marlo, and Carole teamed up with Peter H. Reynolds and his FableVision Team to wave the "design wand" to make the book even more delicious and speak to new generations who will discover this book.

FableVision Team: Peter H. Reynolds - Executive Creative Director; Erika Welch - Producer; Samantha Wilder Oliver - Art Director; Allie Biondi, Tami Wicinas, YouJin Lee, John Brissette - Illustration and Graphic Design; Brendan Joyce, Creative Consultant.

Running Press Kids
2300 Chestnut Street, Philadelphia, PA 19103-4371
Visit us on the web! www.runningpress.com

Contents

(THE HANDY QUICK-GLANCE HOW-TO-FIND-IT GUIDE)

← Free to move the world to a better place.

Dear You,

Well, hello! How marvelous to see you (again).

If you are a grown-up who first read this book 34 years ago—and are now opening to this page, possibly with your own child snuggled on your lap—welcome back! You look fabulous.

And if you are a child cracking open *Free to Be... You and Me* for the very first time, I'll tell you what I told those original readers: I want you to make a wreck of this book. Bend back the corners on the pages you like best. Write your name on the inside cover or any other place you like. Maybe even put a few stickers on the back. A year from now I want to know that you've touched this book—lived it, loved it, cared for it, and shared it—the way I hope it touches you.

Free to Be... You and Me first began with my niece, Dionne, when she was only five years old. Dionne had asked me to read her a bedtime story, and going though her book shelf I was shocked to discover that most of her storybooks were written to do just that: put her—and her mind—to sleep!

What also surprised me about Dionne's storybooks was that all of the characters in them were so....perfect. They talked alike and acted alike, and practically all of the girls married a prince and the boys slayed a dragon and, of course, lived happily ever after.

But what I was most shocked to see was that all of the books talked about what girls and boys should be, instead of what they could be. That's never a good thing. "Should" is a small and bossy word. "Could" is as big and beautiful as the sky.

So my friends and I got together to create a different kind of book—"a party of a book," we called it—for all of the Dionnes in the world, and all the Donnys, too. We wanted a book that would show every child how special they are. And we wanted to let them know that each of their Happily Ever Afters could and would be different.

And exciting.

And their own.

As you'll soon discover (or rediscover), each of the stories and songs and poems in this book is a little adventure—and the adventure is yours. You can stop and start them whenever you want, or replay them a million times. Sort of like the DVD in your house—only it doesn't plug in. And the best thing is, even when you're not holding the book, you can still play it in your head.

You'll also notice that, even though the characters in this book have names that are different from yours, they're really all about you. That's right—each story, each sentence, each word in *Free to Be … You and Me* was written to remind you that you're the hero of your own life adventure, and that you can write your story any way that you dream it can be.

I often hear from grown ups who were children when they first read *Free to Be*, and, to my delight, they tell me that they now share this book with their own kids (including Dionne who now has two little *Free to Be* boys of her own!). Which brings me to the one thing we have changed in this new edition: the look of the book. Don't get me wrong—we liked the illustrations plenty in the original version, but back then we didn't have things like laptops and Photoshop and 3-D animation—and the only thing you could do with a "mouse" was run away from it and scream.

←— That's me in 1972 with my friends.

So my friends and I thought it was time to make the book look a little more like the world you live in today. We contacted some of the best artists in the world—maybe even a few who have illustrated some of your favorite books—and asked them to retell the stories and poems in their own special way, using their favorite colored pencils and paint brushes and drawing programs. And, just like you, they all had their very own ideas of what a story is all about.

We're thrilled with the images they came up with, and we know you will be, too.

OK, so enough talking. Let's go inside the book—and we'll do it the same way we did it the first time around. Ready? All right… Take a giant step.

May I?

Yes, you may.

Yes, we certainly hope you will.

Lots of Love,
Me (Marlo Thomas)
P.S. Now it's you and me.

Each of the stories and songs and poems in this book is a little ADVENTURE – and the adventure is yours!

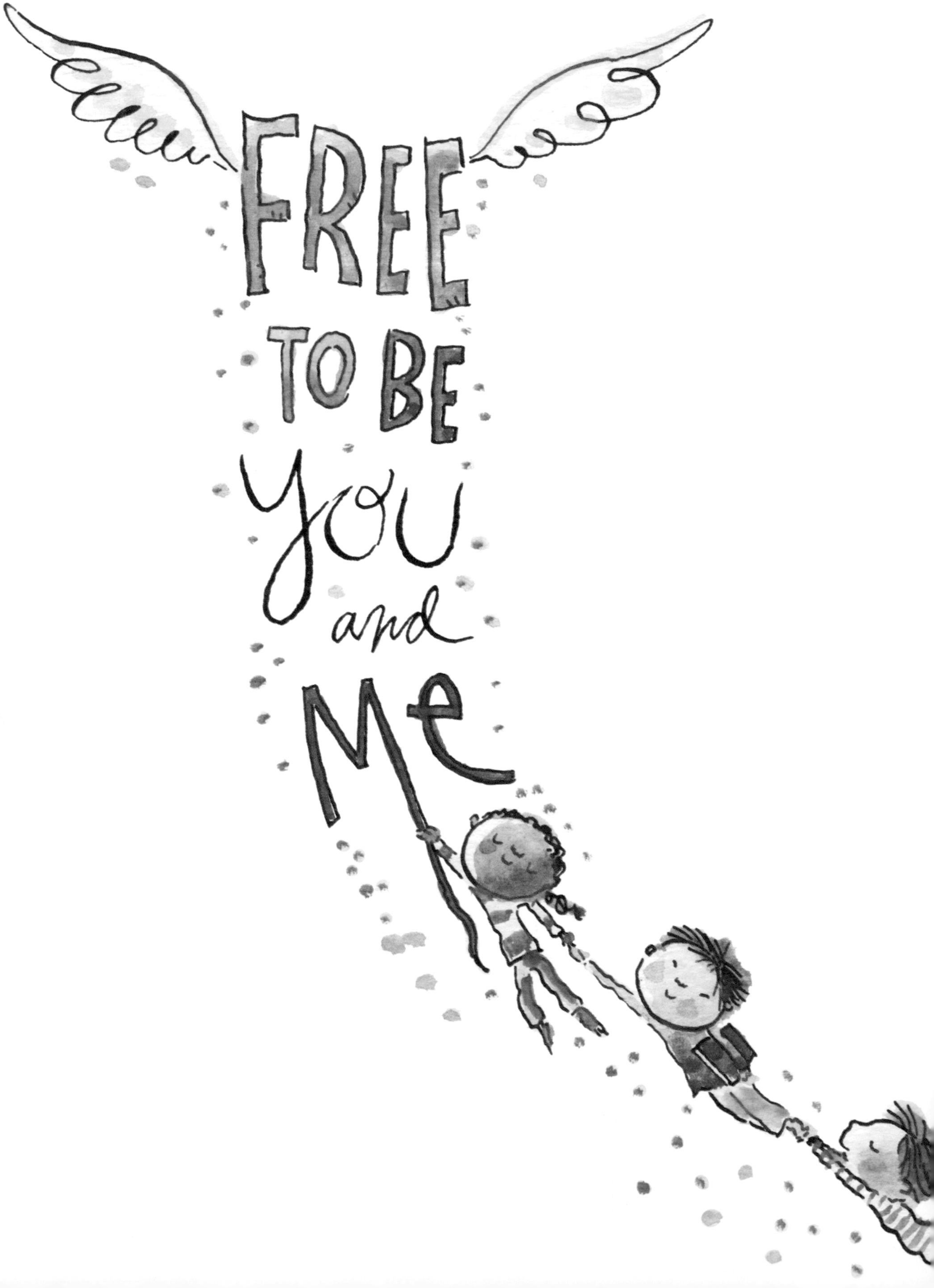
FREE
TO BE
YOU
and
ME

Free to Be... You and Me

Music by Stephen Lawrence
Lyrics by Bruce Hart
Illustrated by Peter H. Reynolds

There's a land that I see
Where the children are free.
And I say it ain't far
To this land, where we are.

Take my hand. Come with me,
Where the children are free.
Come with me, take my hand,
And we'll live...

In a land
Where the river runs free—
(In a land)
Through a green country—
(In a land)
To a shining sea.
And you and me
Are free to be
You and me.

I see a land, bright and clear,
And the time's coming near,
When we'll live in this land,
You and me, hand-in-hand.
Take my hand. Come along,
Lend your voice to my song.
Come along, take my hand.
Sing a song...

For a land
Where the river runs free—
(For a land)
Through the green country—
(For a land)
To a shining sea—
(For a land)
Where the horses run free.
And you and me
Are free to be
You and me.

Every boy in this land
Grows to be his own man.
In this land, every girl
Grows to be her own woman.
Take my hand. Come with me.
Where the children are free.
Come with me. Take my hand,
And we'll run...

To a land
Where the river runs free —
(To a land)
Through a green country —
(To a land)
To a shining sea.
(To a land)
Where the horses run free.
(To a land)
Where the children are free.

And you and me, Are free to be, You and me.
And you and me, Are free to be, You and me.

BOY MEETS GIRL

BY PETER STONE AND CARL REINER
ILLUSTRATED BY JOE MATHIEU
BASED ON PUPPETS CREATED BY WAYLON FLOWERS

18

When We Grow Up

MUSIC BY STEPHEN LAWRENCE
LYRICS BY SHELLEY MILLER
ILLUSTRATED BY LYNN MUNSINGER

When we grow up will I be pretty?
Will you be big and strong?
Will I wear dresses
that show off my knees?
Will you wear trousers twice as long?

•

Well, I don't care if I'm pretty at all
And I don't care if you never get tall
I like what I look like and
you're nice small
We don't have to change at all.

•

When we grow up will I be a lady?
Will you be on the moon?
Well, it might be all right to dance by its light
But I'm gonna get up there soon.

Well, I don't care if I'm pretty at all
And I don't care if you never get tall
I like what I look like and you're nice small
We don't have to change at all.

·

When I grow up I'm going to be happy
And do what I like to do,
Like making noise and making faces
And making friends like you.

·

And when we grow up do you
think we'll see
That I'm still like you
And you're still like me?
I might be pretty
You might grow tall
But we don't have to change at all.

WHAT ARE LITTLE BOYS MADE OF?

BY ELAINE LARON

DRAWING BY SHELBY EASTERLING, AGE 13
ST. JUDE CHILDREN'S RESEARCH HOSPITAL

What are **little boys** made of, made of?
What are little boys made of?
Love and care
And skin and hair
That's what little boys are made of.

What are **little girls** made of, made of?
What are little girls made of?
Care and love
And (SEE ABOVE)
That's what little girls are made of.

Ladies First

BY SHEL SILVERSTEIN

ADAPTED BY MARY RODGERS

Did you hear the one about the little girl who was a "tender sweet young thing?" Well, that's the way she thought of herself. And this tender sweet young thing spent a great deal of time just looking in the mirror, saying,

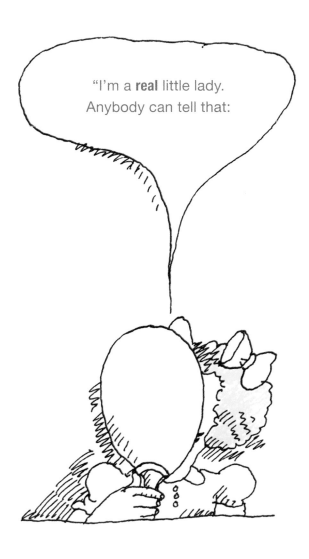

"I'm a **real** little lady.
Anybody can tell that:

"**LADIES first, LADIES first!**"

When she was at the end of the lunch line at school, all she had to say was, "Ladies first, ladies first!" And she'd get right up to the front of the line.

Well, her life went on like that for quite awhile and she wound up having a pretty good time—you know—admiring herself in mirrors, always getting to be first in line, and stuff like that.

And then one day she went exploring with a whole group of other people through the wilds of a deep and beastly jungle. As she went along through the tangled trails and the prickly vines, she would say things like,

"I have got to be careful of my lovely dress and my nice white socks and my shiny, shiny shoes and my curly, curly locks, so would somebody please clear the way for me?"

And **they did**.

Or sometimes she'd say,

"What do you *mean* there aren't enough mangoes to go around and I'll have to share my mango because I was the last one across that icky river full of crocodiles and snakes? No matter how last I am, it's still

'LADIES first, LADIES first!'

so hand over a whole mango, please."

And **they did**.

Well, then, guess what happened? Out of nowhere, the exploring party was seized, grabbed up by a bunch of hungry tigers, and these tigers tied all the people up and dragged them back to their tiger lair where they sniffed around, trying to decide what would make the best dinner.

27

And so she was.

And mighty tasty, too!

Don't Dress Your Cat in an Apron

BY DAN GREENBURG

ILLUSTRATED BY TONY DITERLIZZI

Don't dress your cat in an apron

Just 'cause he's learning to bake.

Don't put your horse
in a nightgown

Just 'cause he can't stay awake.

Don't dress your snake
in a muu-muu

Just 'cause he's off on a cruise.

Don't dress your whale in galoshes

If she really prefers overshoes.

•

A person should wear
what he wants to

And not just what other folks say.

A person should do
what she likes to—

A person's a person that way.

Parents are People

BY CAROL HALL

ILLUSTRATED BY HENRY COLE

Mommies are people.
People with children.
When mommies were little
They used to be girls,
Like some of you,
But then they grew.

And now mommies are women,
Women with children,
Busy with children
And things that they do.
There are a lot of things
A lot of mommies can do.

Some mommies are ranchers
Or poetry makers
Or doctors or teachers
Or cleaners or bakers.

Some mommies drive taxis
Or sing on TV.
Yes, mommies can be
Almost anything they want to be.

They can't be grandfathers . . .
Or daddies . . .

Daddies are people.
People with children.
When daddies were little
They used to be boys,
Like some of you,
But then they grew.

And now daddies are men,
Men with children,
Busy with children
And things that they do.
There are a lot of things
A lot of daddies can do.

Some daddies are writers
Or grocery sellers
Or painters or welders
Or funny joke tellers.
Some daddies play cello
Or sail on the sea.
Yes, daddies can be
Almost anything they want to be.

They can't be grandmas . . .
Or mommies . . .

Parents are people.
People with children.
When parents were little
They used to be kids,
Like all of you.
But then they grew.

And now parents are grown-ups,
Grown-ups with children,
Busy with children
And things that they do.
There are a lot of things
A lot of mommies
And a lot of daddies
And a lot of parents
Can do.

The Pain AND THE GREAT ONE

A pair of poems

BY JUDY BLUME

ILLUSTRATED BY JIMMY PICKERING

My brother's a pain.
He won't get out of bed
In the morning.
My mother has to carry him
Into the kitchen.
He opens his eyes
When he smells
His Sugar Pops.

He should get dressed himself.
He's six.
He's in first grade.
But he's so pokey
Daddy has to help him
Or he'd never be ready in time
And he'd miss the bus.

My sister thinks she's so great
Just because she's older.
Which makes Daddy
and Mom think
She's really smart.
But I know the truth.
My sister's a jerk.

She thinks she's great
Just because she can
Play the piano.
And you can tell
The songs are real ones.
But I like my songs better.
Even if nobody
Ever heard them before.

He cries if I
Leave without him.
Then Mom gets mad
And yells at me.
Which is another reason why
My brother's a pain.

He's got to be first
To show Mom
His school work.
She says *ooh* and *aah*
Over all his pictures.
Which aren't great at all
But just ordinary
First grade stuff.

At dinner he picks
At his food.
He's not supposed
To get dessert
If he doesn't
Eat his meat.
But he always
Gets it anyway.

My sister thinks she's so great
Just because she can work
The electric can opener.
Which means she gets
To feed the cat.
Which means the cat
Likes her better than me
Just because she feeds her.

My sister thinks she's so great
Just because Aunt Diana lets
Her watch the baby.
And tells her how much
The baby likes *her*.

And all the time
The baby is sleeping
In my dresser drawer.
Which my mother has fixed up
Like a bed
For when the baby
Comes to visit.

And I'm not supposed
To touch him
Even if he's
In *my* drawer.
And gets changed
On *my* bed.

When he takes a bath
My brother the pain
Powders the whole bathroom
And he never gets his face clean.
Daddy says
He's learning to
Take care of himself.
I say,
He's a slob!

My brother the pain
Is two years younger than me.
Sow how come
He gets to stay up
As late as I do?
Which isn't really late enough
For somebody in third grade
Anyway.

I asked Mom and Daddy
about that.
They said,
"You're right.
You *are* older.
You *should* stay up later."

My sister thinks she's so great
Just because she can
Remember phone numbers.
And when she dials
She never gets
The wrong person.

And when she has friends over
They build whole cities
Out of blocks.
I like to be garbage man.
I zoom my trucks all around.
So what if I knock down
Some of the buildings?

"It's not fair
That she always gets
To use the blocks!"
I told my mother and father.

They said,
"You're right.
Today you can use the blocks
All by yourself."

So they tucked the Pain
Into bed.
I couldn't wait
For the fun to begin.
I waited
And waited
And waited.
But Daddy and Mom
Just sat there
Reading books.

Finally I shouted,
"I'm going to bed!"

"We thought you wanted
To stay up later,"
They said.

"I did.
But without the Pain
There's nothing to do!"

"Remember that tomorrow,"
My mother said.
And she smiled.

"I'm going to build a whole city
Without you!"
I told the Great One.

"Go ahead," she said.
"Go build a whole state
without me.
See if I care!"

So I did.
I built a whole country
All by myself.
Only it's not the funnest thing
To play blocks alone.
Because when I zoomed
my trucks
And knocked down buildings
Nobody cared but me!

"Remember that tomorrow,"
Mom said, when I told her
I was through playing blocks.

But the next day
My brother was a pain again.
When I got a phone call
He danced all around me
Singing stupid songs
At the top of his lungs.
Why does he have to act that way?

And why does he always
Want to be a garbage man
When I build a city
Out of blocks?
Who needs him
Knocking down buildings
With his dumb old trucks!

And I would really like to know
Why the cat sleeps on the Pain's bed
Instead of mine.
Especially since I am the one
Who feeds her.
That is the meanest thing of all!

I don't understand
How my mother can say
The Pain is lovable.
She's always kissing him
And hugging him
And doing disgusting things
Like that.
And my father says
The Pain is just what
They always wanted.

YUCK!

I think they love him better than me.

But the next day
We went swimming.
I can't stand my sister
When we go swimming.
She thinks she's so great
Just because she can swim and dive

And isn't afraid
To put her face
In the water.
I'm scared to put mine in
So she calls me *baby*.

Which is why
I have to
Spit water at her
And pull her hair
And even pinch her
Sometimes.

And I don't think it's fair
For Daddy and Mom to yell at me
Because none of it's my fault.
But they yell anyway.

Then my mother hugs my sister
And messes with her hair
And does other disgusting things
Like that.
And my father says
The Great One is just what
They always wanted.

I think they love her better than me.

39

Sisters and Brothers

Music by Stephen Lawrence
Lyrics by Bruce Hart
Illustrated by Peter H. Reynolds

SISTERS AND BROTHERS, BROTHERS AND SISTERS! AIN'T WE EV'RYONE? BROTHERS AND SISTERS, SISTERS AND BROTHERS, EV'RY FATHER'S DAUGHTER, EV'RY MOTHER'S SON

Ain't we lucky ev'rybody being ev'rybody's brother?
Ain't we lucky ev'rybody, lookin' out for one another?
Ain't we happy ev'rybody being ev'rybody's sister?
Ain't we happy ev'rybody, lookin' out for Mister Mister?
Ain't we lucky? (ain't we?) Ain't we happy? (ain't we?)

Ain't we lucky? (ain't we?) Ain't we happy? (ain't we?)

Brothers and sisters, sisters and brothers, each and ev'ryone
Sisters and brothers, brothers and sisters,
ev'ry mother's daughter, every father's son.
Ain't we lucky ev'rybody being ev'rybody's brother?
Ain't we lucky ev'rybody, lookin' out for one another?
Ain't we happy ev'rybody being ev'rybody's sister?
Ain't we happy ev'rybody, lookin' out for Mister Mister?
Ain't we lucky? (ain't we?) Ain't we happy? (ain't we?)

Ain't we lucky? (ain't we?) Ain't we happy? (ain't we?)

Sisters and brothers, brothers and sisters, ain't we ev'ryone?
Brothers and sisters, sisters and brothers, ev'ry mother's son
Brothers and sisters, sisters and brothers, each and ev'ryone
Sisters and brothers, brothers and sisters,
ev'ry mother's daughter, every father's son.

the SOUTHPAW

BY JUDITH VIORST

ILLUSTRATED BY PETER H. REYNOLDS

From: Janet

To: Richard

Dear Richard,

Don't invite me to your birthday party because I'm not coming. And give back the Disneyland sweatshirt I said you could wear. If I'm not good enough to play on your team, I'm not good enough to be friends with.

Your former friend,
Janet

P.S. I hope when you go to the dentist he finds 20 cavities.

On Apr 24, at 3:05 PM, Richard wrote:

Dear Janet,

Here is your stupid Disneyland sweatshirt, if that's how you're going to be. I want my comic books now-finished or not. No girl has ever played on the Mapes Street baseball team, and as long as I'm captain, no girl ever will.

Your former friend,
Richard

P.S. I hope when you go for your checkup you need a tetanus shot.

From: Janet
To: Richard

Dear Richard,

I'm changing my goldfish's name from Richard to Stanley. Don't count on my vote for class president next year. Just because I'm a member of the ballet club doesn't mean I'm not a terrific ballplayer.

Your former friend,
Janet

P.S. I see you lost your first game 28-0.

On Apr 25, at 3:15 PM, Richard wrote:

Dear Janet,

I'm not saving any more seats for you on the bus. For all I care you can stand the whole way to school. Why don't you just forget about baseball and learn something nice like knitting?

Your former friend,
Richard

P.S. Wait until Wednesday.

From: Janet

To: Richard

Dear Richard,

My father said I could call someone to go with us for a ride and hot-fudge sundaes. In case you didn't notice, I didn't call you.

Your former friend,
Janet

P.S. I see you lost your second game, 34-0.

On May 1, at 4:04 PM, Richard wrote:

Dear Janet,

Remember when I took the laces out of my blue-and-white sneakers and gave them to you? I want them back.

Your former friend,
Richard

P.S. Wait until Friday.

From: Janet

To: Richard

Dear Richard,

Congratulations on your unbroken record. Eight straight losses, wow: I understand you're the laughing stock of New Jersey.

Your former friend,
Janet

P.S. Why don't you and your team forget about baseball and learn something nice like knitting maybe?

On May 3, at 4:13 PM, Richard wrote:

Dear Janet,

Here's the silver horseback riding trophy that you gave me. I don't think I want to keep it anymore.

Your former friend,
Richard

P.S. I didn't think you'd be the kind who'd kick a man when he's down.

From: Janet

To: Richard

Dear Richard,

I wasn't kicking exactly. I was kicking back.

Your former friend,
Janet

P.S. In case you were wondering, my batting average is .345.

On May 4, at 4:22 PM, Richard wrote:

Dear Janet,

Alfie is having his tonsils out tomorrow. We might be able to let you catch next week.

Richard

From: Janet

To: Richard

Dear Richard,

I pitch.

Janet

On May 12, at 4:25 PM, Richard wrote:

Dear Janet,

Joel is moving to Kansas and Danny sprained his
wrist. How about a permanent place in the outfield?

Richard

From: Janet

To: Richard

Dear Richard,

I pitch.

Janet

On May 20, at 4:32 PM, Richard wrote:

Dear Janet,

Ronnie caught the chicken pox and Leo broke his toe
and Elwood has these stupid violin lessons. I'll
give you first base, and that's my final offer.

Richard

From: Janet

To: Richard

Dear Richard,

Susan Reilly plays first base, Marilyn Jackson catches, Ethel Kahn plays center field, I pitch. It's a package deal.

Janet

P.S. Sorry about your 12-game losing streak.

On May 21, at 4:55 PM, Richard wrote:

Dear Janet,

Please! Not Marilyn Jackson.

Richard

From: Janet

To: Richard

Dear Richard,

Nobody ever said that I was unreasonable. How about Lizzie
Martindale instead?

Janet

On May 23, at 5:05 PM, Richard wrote:

Dear Janet,

At least could you call your goldfish Richard
again?

Your friend,

Richard

the Old Woman Who Lived in a Shoe

BY JOYCE JOHNSON

ILLUSTRATED BY DAVID CATROW

There was an old woman
who lived in a shoe,
And all her grandchildren
played there too.

She laughed at their jokes
(when they were funny)
And kept a green jar
of bubblegum money.
She rode with them
on the carousel
And played Monopoly very well.

She taught them to paint
and how to bake bread.
She read them riddles
and tucked them in bed.
She taught them to sing
and how to climb trees.
She patched their jeans
and bandaged their knees.

She remembered the way
she'd felt as a child,
The dreams she'd had
of lands that were wild,
Of mountains to climb
of villains to fight,
Of plays and poems
she'd wanted to write.

She remembered all
she'd wanted to do
Before she grew up
and lived in the shoe.

There was an old woman
who lived in a shoe
And lived in the dreams
she'd had once too.
She told those she loved,
"Children be bold
Then you'll grow up
But never grow old."

My Dog is a PLUMBER

BY DAN GREENBURG

ILLUSTRATED BY DOUG TAYLOR

My dog is a plumber, he must be a boy.

Although I must tell you his favorite toy

Is a little play stove with pans and with pots

Which he really must like, 'cause
he plays with it lots.

So perhaps he's a girl,
which kind of makes sense,

Since he can't throw a ball and
he can't climb a fence.

But neither can Dad, and I know *he's* a man,

And Mom is a woman, and
she drives a van.

Maybe the problem is in trying to tell

Just what someone is by what he does well.

Dudley Pippin and the Principal

BY PHIL RESSNER
ILLUSTRATED BY ARNOLD LOBEL

One day at school the sand table tipped over. Dudley Pippin's teacher thought Dudley had done it and she made him stay a long time after school. Dudley was very angry. On his way home he met the principal, who had a long nose and fierce eyes.

"Hello, Dudley," the principal said. "People are saying you tipped over the sand table at school today."

Dudley just shook his head, because he couldn't say anything. It wasn't fair.

The principal said, "Didn't you do it?"

Dudley shook his head.

"I *knew* you didn't do it," the principal said. "Your teacher must have made a mistake. It wasn't fair. We'll have to do something about it, first thing tomorrow morning."

Dudley nodded.

"I bet you'd like to cry," the principal said.

"No," Dudley said, and began to cry. "Boo-wah, hoo-wah," he cried. "Boo-hooh, wah-hoo, boo-hoo-wah." He cried a long time.

"That's fine," the principal said when Dudley was through.

"I'm sorry," Dudley said.

"What for?" the principal said. "You did that very well."

"But only sissies cry," Dudley said.

"A sissy," the principal said, "is somebody who *doesn't* cry because he's afraid people will call him a sissy if he *does*."

"I'm all mixed up." Dudley said.

"Of course," the principal said. "Why should *you* be any different from everybody else? Most people spend their whole lives trying to get unmixed up."

Then he took a little blue flute out of his pocket. "Say," he said. "Just listen to this nice tune I learned yesterday; it's lovely."

And he began to play, and the music was sad and joyous and it filled the quiet street and went out over the darkling trees and the whole world.

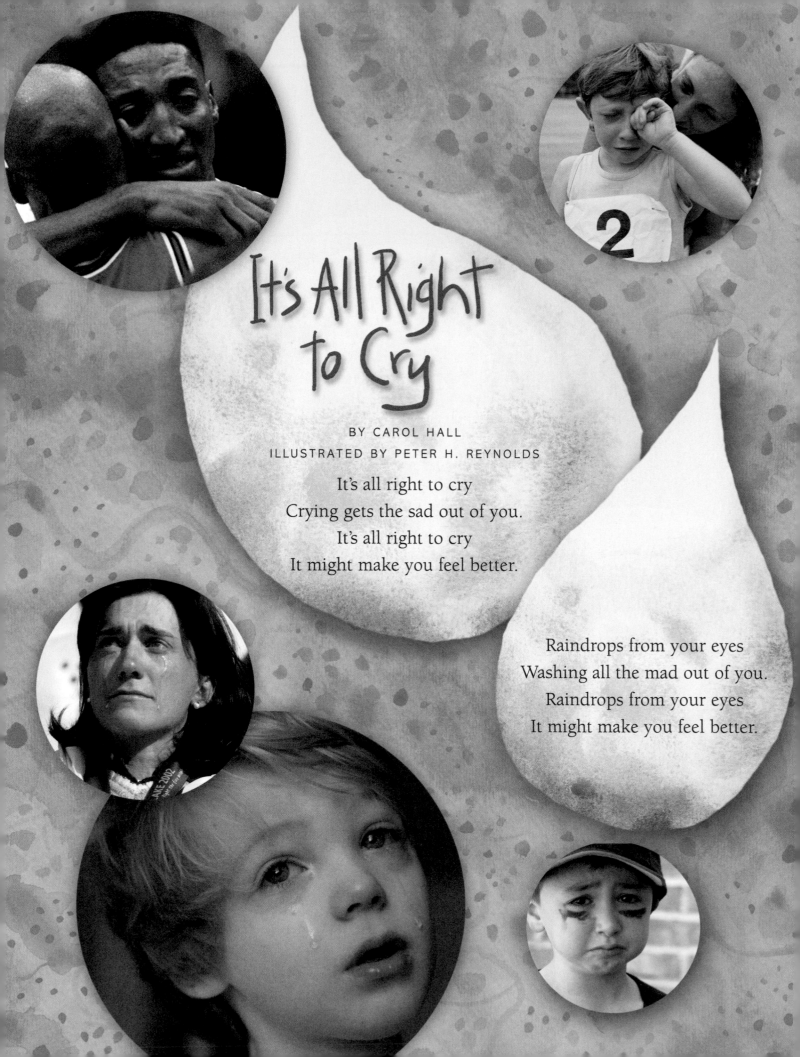

It's All Right to Cry

BY CAROL HALL

ILLUSTRATED BY PETER H. REYNOLDS

It's all right to cry
Crying gets the sad out of you.
It's all right to cry
It might make you feel better.

Raindrops from your eyes
Washing all the mad out of you.
Raindrops from your eyes
It might make you feel better.

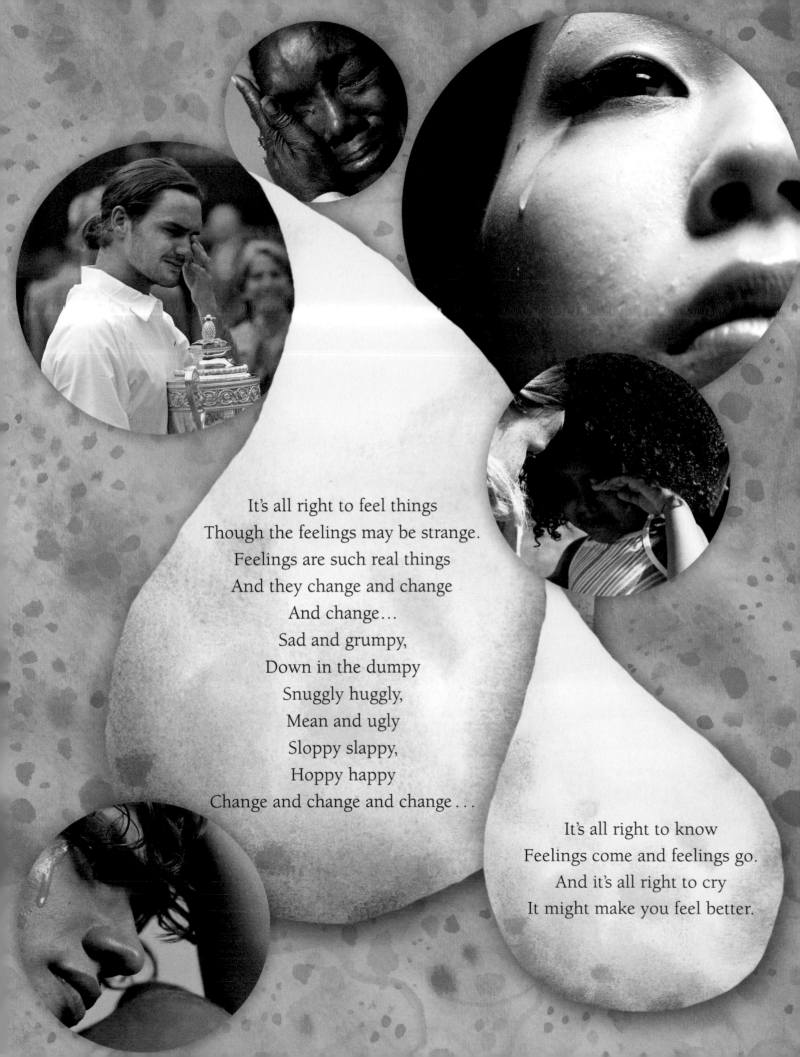

It's all right to feel things
Though the feelings may be strange.
Feelings are such real things
And they change and change
And change…
Sad and grumpy,
Down in the dumpy
Snuggly huggly,
Mean and ugly
Sloppy slappy,
Hoppy happy
Change and change and change . . .

It's all right to know
Feelings come and feelings go.
And it's all right to cry
It might make you feel better.

William's Doll

MUSIC BY MARY RODGERS   LYRICS BY SHELDON HARNICK
ADAPTED FROM THE BOOK, *WILLIAM'S DOLL*
BY CHARLOTTE ZOLOTOW
ILLUSTRATED BY LEUYEN PHAM

When my friend William was five years old he wanted a doll to hug and hold.

"A doll," said William, "is what I need to wash and clean and dress and feed; a doll to give a bottle to and put to bed when day is through; and any time my doll gets ill, I'll take good care of it," said my friend Bill.

"A doll! A doll! William wants a doll!"

"Don't be a sissy," said his best friend Ed. "Why should a boy want to play with a doll?"

"Dolls are for girls," said his cousin Fred. "Don't be a jerk," said his older brother.

"I know what to do," said his father to his mother. So his father bought him a basketball, a badminton set, and that's not all: A bag of marbles, a baseball glove, and all the things a boy would love. And Bill was good at ev'ry game, enjoyed them all but all the same when Billy's father praised his skill, "Can I please have a doll now?" said my friend Bill.

56

"A doll! A doll! William wants a doll!" "A doll! A doll! William wants a doll!"

Then William's grandma arrived one day and wanted to know what he liked to play. And Bill said, "Baseball's my fav'rite game. I like to play, but all the same, I'd give my bat and ball and glove to have a doll that I could love."

"How very wise," his grandma said. Said Bill, "But ev'ry one says this instead!:

"A doll! A doll! William wants a doll!" "A doll! A doll! William wants a doll!"

So William's grandma, as I've been told, bought William a doll to hug and hold.

And William's father began to frown but grandma smiled and calmed him down, explaining: "William wants a doll so when he has a baby some day he'll know how to dress it, put diapers on double, and gently caress it to bring up a bubble, and care for his baby as ev'ry good father should learn to do.

William has a doll! William has a doll!
'Cause some day he may want to be a father, too."

The Field

BY ANNE ROIPHE

ILLUSTRATED BY JERRY PINKNEY

Once there was a great field. At one edge of the field there were trees and bushes and on the other a thin country road that curved about untraveled for many miles.

In the field were rocks, high gray piles of stone, good for the climbing, hiding, and exploring games of children.

In the middle of the field there was a tree, a single tree that had been growing for more than a hundred years. It was gnarled and its branches spread in many directions. The children from the neighboring villages would use the tree for home base in their games of tag and hide-and-go-seek.

The field lay just between the Kingdoms of Aura and Ghent. Both kings claimed the field even though it was bare except for the rocks and the tree and the children who played in it.

"Mine," said the King of Aura, politely.

"Mine," answered the King of Ghent in a louder voice.

Then the people of both countries began to say ugly things about each other.

And soon two armies gathered—one on each side of the field.

The battle began. The Aurians were camped by the bushes and the trees and the Ghentians were over on the other side of the road.

In the tree in the middle of the field a robin had built her nest of twigs and grass. She had woven it together and now the nest hidden by summer leaves held three blue eggs. Carefully, the mother sat on her eggs even though the arrows whizzed past the tree and the shotguns made sounds of thunder and there was the sound of screaming when soldiers were hurt or frightened. The bird stayed on her nest although there was crying and singing and shouting as the men moved up to the foot of the tree and then retreated.

One morning when the soldiers were starting to shoot at each other again, the robin flew down to the grass and unearthed a worm. As she pulled it from the soil, the guns pounded the ground and the soldiers moved up and down, hiding and crawling in the thick grass, and there was smoke in the air and blood on the rocks where the children had played.

As the robin was flying back to her nest an arrow with a sharp tip flew past the crouching soldiers and pierced the throat of the bird. Her wings fluttered for a moment and then she fell like a heavy stone. Only one soldier saw her fall.

Then a shell from the king's prize cannon boomed across the field and landed not far from the tree.

The earth shook and the tree trembled and the branches wavered and the nest with the three small eggs fell to the ground.

The young soldier watched the nest fall. He crawled over the rocks and the twigs and found the three small eggs unbroken. Not even a crack was on the shells.

The soldier put his shotgun down on the ground. He took off his iron gray helmet, and turning it over, he filled it with grass and a dandelion and some clover. He carefully placed the nest in the matted grass and cradled the helmet in his arms. He sat for awhile watching the eggs in his helmet.

The commanding officer came by and saw one of his soldiers sitting down.

"Come on soldier, let's go . . . put your helmet on."

The young man, carrying his helmet, reached for his gun and started forward.

"Put your helmet on," the officer shouted.

There was a pause as the soldier looked down at the eggs.

"I can't sir," he said.

"There's no such thing as can't in this man's army," yelled the officer. "Put your helmet on your head."

The soldier put down his gun.

"I think," he said in a very quiet voice, "I think I'm going home now sir."

The commanding officer turned red in the face but the young man, carefully holding his helmet under his arm, turned around and walked off the field, past the bushes and trees.

On his way home the three eggs broke open and three small wet birds opened their tiny beaks for food. The soldier stopped. He gathered some berries from a nearby bush and offered them gently to each bird in turn. The soldier smiled. Then the birds settled down, resting on one another, and fell asleep.

THREE WISHES

BY LUCILLE CLIFTON

ILLUSTRATED BY CHRISTOPHER MYERS

Everybody knows there's such a thing as luck. Like when a good man be the first person to come in your house on the New Year Day you have a good year, but I know somethin better than that! Find a penny on the New Year Day with your birthday on it, and you can make three wishes on it and the wishes will come true! It happened to me.

First wish was when I found the penny. Me and Victorius Richardson was goin for a walk, wearin our new boots we got for Christmas and our new hat and scarf sets when I saw somethin all shiny in the snow.

Victor say, "What is that, Lena?"

"Look like some money," I say, and I picked it up. It was a penny with my birthday on it. 1998.

Victor say, "Look like you in for some luck now, Lena. That's a lucky penny for you. What you gonna wish?"

"Well, one thing I do wish is it wasn't so cold," I say just halfway jokin. And the sun come out. Just then.

Well, that got me thinkin. Me and Victor started back to my house both of us thinkin bout the penny and what if there really is such a thing and what to wish in case. Mama was right in the living room when we got to the house.

"How was the walk, Nobie?"

"Fine thank you, Mama," I say.

"Fine thank you, ma'am," Victor say as we went back to the kitchen.

My name is Zenobia after somebody in the Bible. My name is Zenobia and everybody calls me Nobie. Everybody but Victor. He calls me Lena after Lena Horne and when I get grown I'm goin to Hollywood and sing in the movies and Victorius is gonna go with me 'cause he my best friend. That's his real name.

Back in the kitchen it was nice and warm 'cause the stove was lit and Mama had opened the oven door. Me and Victor sat at the table talkin soft so nobody would hear.

"You get two more wishes, Lena."

"You really think there's something to it?"

"What you mean, didn't you see how the sun come ridin out soon as you said about it bein too cold?"

"You really think so?"

"Man, don't you believe nothin?"

"I just don't believe everything like you do, that's all!"

"Well, you just simple!"

"Who you callin simple?"

"Simple you, that's who, simple Zenobia!"

I jumped up from the table, "Man, I wish you would get out of here!" and Victor jumped up and ran out of the room and grabbed his coat and ran out of the house. Just then.

Well, I'm tellin you! I just sat back down at the table and shook my head. I had just about wasted another wish! I didn't have but one more left!

Mama came into the kitchen lookin for me. "Zenobia, what was the matter with Victorius?" She call me Zenobia when she kind of mad.

"We was just playin, Mama."

"Well, why did he run out of here like that?"

"I don't know Mama, that's how Victor is."

"Well, I hope you wasn't bein unfriendly to him Zenobia, 'cause I know how you are too."

Yes, ma'am. Mama, what would you wish for if you could have anything you wanted in the whole wide world?"

Mama sat down at the table and started playin with the salt shaker. "What you mean, Nobie?"

"I mean, if you could have yourself one wish, what would it be for?"

Mama put the salt back on a straight line with the pepper and got the look on her face like when she tellin me the old wise stuff.

"Good friends, Nobie. That's what we need in this world. Good friends." Then she went back to playin with the table.

Well, I didn't think she was gonna say that! Usually when I hear the grown people talkin bout different things they want, they be talkin bout money or a good car or somethin like that. Mama always do come up with a surprise!

I got up and got my coat and went to sit out on the step. I started thinkin bout ole Victor and all the stuff me and him used to do. Goin to the movies and practicin my singin and playin touch ball and stick ball and one time we found a rock with a whole lotta shiny stuff in it look just like a diamond. One time me and him painted a picture of the whole school. He was really a good friend to me. Never told one of my secrets. Hard to find friends like that.

"Wish I still had a good friend," I whispered to myself, holdin the penny real tight and feelin all sorry for myself.

And who do you think come bustin down the street grinnin at me? Just then!

Yeah, there's such a thing as luck. Lot of people think they know different kinds of luck but this thing bout the penny is really real. I know 'cause just like I say, it happened to me.

No One Else

BY ELAINE LARON

Now, someone else can tell you how
To multiply by three
And someone else can tell you how
To spell Schenectady
And someone else can tell you how
To ride a two-wheeled bike
But no one else, no, no one else
Can tell you what to like.

An engineer can tell you how
To run a railroad train
A map can tell you where to find
The capital of Spain
A book can tell you all the names
Of every star above
But no one else, no, no one else
Can tell you who to love.

Your aunt Louise can tell you how
To plant a pumpkin seed
Your cousin Frank can tell you how
To catch a centipede
Your Mom and Dad can tell you how
To brush between each meal
But no one else, no, no one else
Can tell you how to feel.

What I Like...
Willow Trees
My Pillow
My Family
Buttered Toast
Rain
Helping People
Recycling

← Free to be a dancer.

For how you feel is how you feel
And all the whole world through
No one else, no, no one else
Knows *that* as well as YOU!

67

GLAD TO HAVE A FRIEND LIKE YOU

BY CAROL HALL

ILLUSTRATED BY PETER H. REYNOLDS

Jill told Bill
That it was lots of fun to cook.
Bill told Jill
That she could bait a real fish hook.

So they made ooey gooey
Chocolate cake
Sticky licky
Sugar top
And they gobbled it and giggled.
And they sat by the river
And they fished in the water
And they talked
As the squirmy wormies wiggled,
Singin'

Glad to have a friend like you,
Fair and fun and skippin' free.
Glad to have a friend like you,
And glad to just be me.

Peg told Greg
She liked to make things out of chairs.
Greg told Peg
Sometimes he still hugged teddy bears.

So they sneaked in the living room
And piled all the pillows up
And made it a rocket ship
To fly in.
And the bears were their girls and boys
And they were the astronauts
Who lived on the moon
With one pet lion,
Singin'

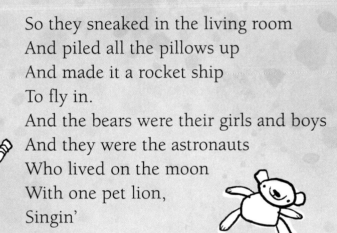

Glad to have a friend like you,
Fair and fun and skippin' free.
Glad to have a friend like you,
And glad to just be me.

Pearl told Earl
That they could do a secret code.
Earl told Pearl
There was free ice cream when it snowed.

So they sent funny letters
Which contained mystery messages
And nobody knew just how they
made it.
And they raised up the window
And they scooped all the snow together,
Put milk and sugar in and ate it,
Singin'

Glad to have a friend like you,
Fair and fun and skippin' free.
Glad to have a friend like you,
And glad to just be me.

Zachary's Divorce

BY LINDA SITEA

ILLUSTRATED BY DAN ANDREASON

On this particular Saturday morning Zachary's toes woke up first. They wiggled and wiggled and wiggled in the warm sunlight streaming through the windows. Zachary could feel them wiggling but he couldn't see them because his eyes were still asleep. Next, his arms and mouth woke up and together gave a gigantic stretch and yawn. The yawn sounded something like this: "Aaarrr." Then his whole body woke up and turned over and over, quickly, and before the last turn was done his eyes opened and Zachary was all awake.

Slowly he climbed out of bed and tiptoed across the rug. He moved carefully, so he wouldn't step on the blue and green flowers, only the purple ones, because purple was his favorite color.

He went straight to Mommy's and Daddy's room. He looked at Mommy sleeping in Mommy's and Daddy's bed. He looked at the wood sculptures he had made in school that were nailed into the wall. He looked at the leafy avocado plant that was almost to the ceiling, just the right size for pretending you were an explorer lost in the jungle. Zachary looked at the bookshelves and the easel and Mommy's paintings. He even looked in the closets and under the bed. Daddy was not there.

Next he went into the bathroom. And while he was there he sang a little song:

La la pee dee

La la pee vee

La la pee gee

Daddy was not in the bathroom.

Zachary slid down the stairs on his stomach, bump bump, bump.

He walked back and forth from the living room to the dining room four times and tried to practice his whistling. But no whistle came out, only a puff of wind.

Zachary looked at the bookshelves and his favorite plant that was all purple.

Daddy wasn't in the living room either.

Next Zachary went into the kitchen and there on the wall was his best invention. He turned the handle and the pulley went around and the rope pulled the refrigerator door open. Daddy had helped him build it but it was all his own idea. Daddy and Mommy had said it was a really great idea because you could open the refrigerator door without walking all the way over to it. Zachary closed the door now. He didn't feel like any orange juice this morning. No Daddy in the kitchen.

Zachary went back into the living room and sat on the big chair. He pulled Mommy's patchwork quilt over him and settled in. It was usually a very happy patchwork quilt with every color you could think of in it. But it didn't seem so happy lately.

The morning is a very sad time if you have a divorce, Zachary thought. Having a divorce meant that you woke up in the morning and your Daddy was not there because now Daddy lived in another house. Then Zachary thought of Amy who was in school with him. And he remembered how Amy's divorce meant that she woke up in the morning and her Daddy was there but not her Mommy. He wondered how grown-ups decided which kind of divorce to give you, the Mommy kind or the Daddy kind. Then he tried to figure out, if he could choose, which he would rather have, the Mommy kind or the Daddy kind. But it gave him a headache just to think about it.

Zachary stared out the window. "The morning is a very sad time when you have a divorce," Zachary said out loud.

"I know how you feel. Sometimes the morning is very sad for me too," said Mommy, standing on the bottom step. Mommy was wearing her blue T-shirt and the dungarees Zachary liked best of all—the ones with the bright purple paint on them.

Mommy came and cuddled into the big chair with Zachary and pulled the patchwork quilt over her too.

Zachary whispered, "Mommy tell me the story again about why I got a divorce."

Mommy hugged Zachary very hard and then said: "It's not your divorce Zachary, it's Daddy's and mine. We decided we would be happier if we lived apart from each other. You musn't think it's because of anything you did wrong, because it isn't. Daddy and I have always loved you very much and always will. And remember, you see Daddy a lot and sleep over at his house a lot too."

Zachary snuggled closer to Mommy.

"Do you think Daddy is sometimes sad in the morning too?" Zachary asked.

"Yes, I think he is," said Mommy. "It's okay to be sad. This is a very new thing that has happened to us. But really, as time passes, we'll all get used to the divorce and we'll be less and less and less sad."

"Let's go get some orange juice," Zachary shouted, and ran into the kitchen.

As he turned the pulley handle to open the refrigerator, Zachary pretended time was passing with each turn. And with each turn, he told himself that soon he would feel less and less and less sad.

Helping

BY SHEL SILVERSTEIN
ILLUSTRATED BY MONICA SHEEHAN

Agatha Fry she made a pie, and Christopher John helped bake it.

Christopher John he mowed the lawn, and Agatha Fry helped rake it.

Zachary Zugg took out the rug, and Jennifer Joy helped shake it.

And Jennifer Joy she made a toy, and Zachary Zugg helped break it.

And some kind of help is the kind of help that helping's all about.

And some kind of help is the kind of help we all can do without.

The Sun and the Moon

BY ELAINE LARON
DRAWINGS BY EVA MARIE
AND MIA ANGELA CONNELL, AGE 4

(with a little help from Peter H. Reynolds)

The sun is filled with shining light
It blazes far and wide
The Moon reflects the sunlight back
But has no light inside.

I think I'd rather be the sun
That shines so bold and bright
Than be the Moon, that only glows
With someone else's light.

ATALANTA

BY BETTY MILES

ILLUSTRATED BY BARBARA BASCOVE

Once upon a time, not long ago, there lived a princess named Atalanta, who could run as fast as the wind.

She was so bright, and so clever, and could build things and fix things so wonderfully, that many young men wished to marry her.

"What shall I do?" said Atalanta's father, who was a powerful king. "So many young men want to marry you, and I don't know how to choose."

"You don't have to choose, Father," Atalanta said. "I will choose. And I'm not sure that I will choose to marry anyone at all."

"Of course you will," said the king. "Everybody gets married. It is what people do."

"But," Atalanta told him, with a toss of her head, "I intend to go out and see the world. When I come home, perhaps I will marry and perhaps I will not."

The king did not like this at all. He was a very ordinary king; that is, he was powerful and used to having his own way. So he did not answer Atalanta, but simply told her, "I have decided how to choose the young man you will marry. I will hold a great race, and the winner—the swiftest, fleetest young man of all—will win the right to marry you."

Now Atalanta was a clever girl as well as a swift runner. She saw that she might win both the argument and the race—provided that she herself could run in the race, too. "Very well," she said. "But you must let me race along with the others. If I am not the winner, I will accept the wishes of the young man who is."

The king agreed to this. He was pleased; he would have his way, marry off his daughter, and enjoy a fine day of racing as well. So he directed his messengers to travel throughout the kingdom announcing the race with its wonderful prize: the chance to marry the bright Atalanta.

As the day of the race drew near, flags were raised in the streets of the town, and banners were hung near the grassy field where the race would be run. Baskets of ripe plums and peaches, wheels of cheese, ropes of sausages and onions, and loaves of crusty bread were gathered for the crowds.

Meanwhile, Atalanta herself was preparing for the race. Each day at dawn, dressed in soft green trousers and a shirt of yellow silk, she went to the field in secret and ran across it—slowly at first, then fast and faster, until she could run the course more quickly than anyone had ever run it before.

As the day of the race grew nearer, young men began to crowd into the town. Each was sure he could win the prize, except for one; that was Young John, who lived in the town. He saw Atalanta day by day as she bought nails and wood to make a pigeon house, or chose parts for her telescope, or laughed with her friends. Young John saw the princess only from a distance, but near enough to know how bright and clever she was. He wished very much to race with her, to win, and to earn the right to talk with her and become her friend.

"For surely," he said to himself, "it is not right for Atalanta's father to give her away to the winner of the race. Atalanta herself must choose the person she wants to marry, or whether she wishes to marry at all. Still, if I could only win the race, I would be free to speak to her, and to ask for her friendship."

Each evening, after his studies of the stars and the seas, Young John went to the field in secret and practiced running across it. Night after night, he ran fast as the wind across the twilight field, until he could cross it more quickly than anyone had ever crossed it before.

At last, the day of the race arrived.

Trumpets sounded in the early morning, and the young men gathered at the edge of the field, along with Atalanta herself, the prize they sought. The king and his friends sat in soft chairs, and the townspeople stood along the course.

The king rose to address them all. "Good day," he said to the crowds. "Good luck," he said to the young men. To Atalanta he said, "Good-bye. I must tell you farewell, for tomorrow you will be married."

"I am not so sure of that, Father," Atalanta answered. She was dressed for the race in trousers of crimson and a shirt of silk as blue as the sky, and she laughed as she looked up and down the line of young men.

"Not one of them," she said to herself, "can win the race, for I will run fast as the wind and leave them all behind."

And now a bugle sounded, a flag was dropped, and the runners were off!

The crowds cheered as the young men and Atalanta began to race across the field. At first they ran as a group, but Atalanta soon pulled ahead, with three of the young men close after her. As they neared the halfway point, one young man put on a great burst of speed and seemed to pull ahead for an instant, but then he gasped and fell back. Atalanta shot on.

Soon another young man, tense with the effort, drew near to Atalanta. He reached out as though to touch her sleeve, stumbled for an instant, and lost speed. Atalanta smiled as she ran on. I have almost won, she thought.

But then another young man came near. This was Young John, running like the wind, as steadily and as swiftly as Atalanta herself. Atalanta felt his closeness, and in a sudden burst she dashed ahead.

Young John might have given up at this, but he never stopped running. Nothing at all, thought he, will keep me from winning the chance to speak with Atalanta. And on he ran, swift as the wind, until he ran as her equal, side by side with her, toward the golden ribbon that marked the race's end. Atalanta raced even faster to pull ahead, but Young John was a strong match for her. Smiling with the pleasure of the race, Atalanta and Young John reached the finish line together, and together they broke through the golden ribbon.

Trumpets blew. The crowd shouted and leaped about. The king rose. "Who is that young man?" he asked.

"It is Young John from the town," the people told him.

 ← Free to be a hero!

"Very well. Young John," said the king, as John and Atalanta stood before him, exhausted and jubilant from their efforts. "You have not won the race, but you have come closer to winning than any man here. And so I give you the prize that was promised—the right to marry my daughter."

Young John smiled at Atalanta, and she smiled back. "Thank you, sir," said John to the king, "but I could not possibly marry your daughter unless she wished to marry me. I have run this race for the chance to talk with Atalanta, and, if she is willing, I am ready to claim my prize."

Atalanta laughed with pleasure. "And I," she said to John, "could not possibly marry before I have seen the world. But I would like nothing better than to spend the afternoon with you."

Then the two of them sat and talked on the grassy field, as the crowds went away. They ate bread and cheese and purple plums. Atalanta told John about her telescopes and her pigeons, and John told Atalanta about his globes and his studies of geography. At the end of the day, they were friends.

On the next day, John sailed off to discover new lands. And Atalanta set off to visit the great cities.

By this time, each of them has had wonderful adventures, and seen marvelous sights. Perhaps some day they will be married, and perhaps they will not. In any case, they are friends. And it is certain that they are both living happily ever after.

If Wishes Were Fishes

BY DAVID SLAVIN
ILLUSTRATION BY PETER SIS

"I have a secret," a fish said to me,
"We'll take care of you if you'll take care
    of we."
"Who is 'we?'" I replied, and he said with
    a grin,
"All creatures that live with a tail or a fin."

"We'll carry you, nourish you, feed you,
    and then,
Someday you'll have kids and we'll help
    you again,
But you must do your part,
    all you boys and you girls,
For you are our oysters and we are your pearls."

"But how can I take care of you?" I said back,
"With so many of you, it's numbers I lack,
There's only one me, for what that is worth,
I'm only one person—I'm not the whole earth!"

"Ah, that's where you're wrong,"
    I HEARD THE FISH say,
"You can make a difference, day after day,
Respect Mother Nature, don't take her
    for granted,
Your goodness will spread,
    like seeds that are planted."

"The fish and the plants and the animals know,
There must be a balance in order to grow,
It's people who've gotten things so out
    of whack,
But a person like you
    can put things BACK on track."

"Take just what you need and
    give back where you can,
Make goals for yourself, and then stick
    to a plan,
To live in the world with the lightest
    of touch,
You'll bring joy to life,
    and you'll get back so much."

And I listened and thought,
    and then thought some more,
That lesson he taught me went straight to
    my core,
My heart was on fire, my soul leapt,
    and soon,
My spirit took flight, like a big blue balloon!

"I will watch over you, and you over me,
And working together, we both will be free,
We'll live and let live, and I'll cry out
    that wish,
The wish that I got from the mouth of a fish."

Free to Dream

86

Free to
be a →  ← Free to
mover   Be a
                               SHAKER

Free to Make Some Music

The words in this book can be read silently to yourself with your lips moving or not. Or they can be read aloud to you. Or they can be read by you to your brother, your sister, your cousin, your friends, your cat, your dog, or your hamster. Some of the words in this book are so special you can sing them to music in this section. Singing words is a great way to share them and to remember them. Words attached to music can take wing and soar all around the world.

Note: The music in this book is designed to be played by children of all ages, shapes, sizes, colors, and sexes. Some of the songs are easy to play. Some are more challenging. In either case, chord names above the notes can be used to improvise simpler (or more complex) arrangements of the pieces. Even if you cannot read music, you can enjoy the poems and stories within the musical scores.

FREE TO BE YOU and ME

MUSIC BY STEPHEN LAWRENCE   LYRICS BY BRUCE HART

With spirit

There's a (1) land that I see____ where the chil _ dren are free,__
       (2) land, bright and clear,__ and the time's__ com _ in' near__
       (3) boy in this land__ grows to be___ his own man,__

____ and I say___ it ain't far___ to this land__ from where we are.__
when we'll live__ in this land__ you and me___ hand – in hand.__
in this land,___ ev'ry girl grows__ to be her own wo–man.__

____ Take my hand, come with me,____ where the chil – dren are free_
____ Take my hand, come a – long,___ lend your voice___ to my song.__
____ Take my hand, come with me,___ where the chil – dren are free_

____ Come with me,____ take my hand,___ and we'll live...____
____ Come a – long,____ take my hand,___ sing a song...____
____ Come with me,___ take my hand,___ and we'll run...____

In a land__ where the ri—ver runs free, In a land __ through the green coun—
For a land__ where the ri—ver runs free, For a land __ through the green coun—
To a land__ where the ri—ver runs free, To a land __ through the green coun—

try, In a land __ to a shin—ing sea __ For a land __ where the hor—ses run
try, For a land __ to a shin—ing sea __ For a land __ where the hor—ses run
try, To a land __ to a shin—ing sea __ To a land __ where the chil—dren are

—— And you and me__ are free to be__ you and me.
free,

I see a

Ev — 'ry

Fine
8va lower

When We Grow Up

MUSIC BY STEPHEN LAWRENCE

LYRICS BY SHELLEY MILLER

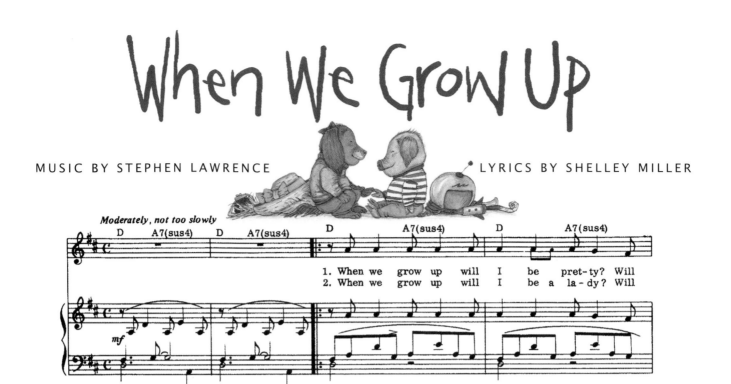

Moderately, not too slowly

1. When we grow up will I be pret-ty? Will
2. When we grow up will I be a la-dy? Will

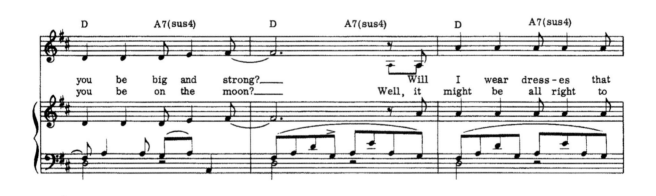

you be big and strong?____ Will I wear dress-es that
you be on the moon?____ Well, it might be all right to

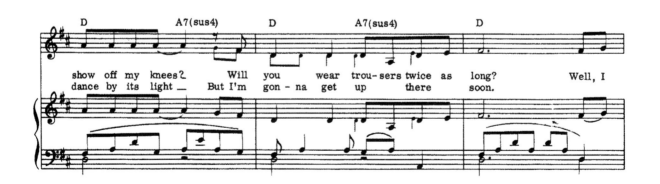

show off my knees? Will you wear trou-sers twice as long? Well, I
dance by its light __ But I'm gon-na get up there soon.

don't   care___ if I'm   pret-ty at all ___   And I   don't   care___   if you

nev - er get tall.___   I   like what I look like, and   you're nice small,   we

don't have to change at   all.

Eb   Bb7(sus4)   Eb   Bb7(sus4)   Eb   Bb7(sus4)

When I grow up I'm

Eb   Bb7(sus4) Eb   Bb7(sus4) Eb   Bb7(sus4) Eb   Bb7(sus4)

go-ing to be hap-py and do what I like to do____ like mak-ing noise and

Eb   Bb7(sus4) Eb   Bb7(sus4) Eb   Ab(sus4)   Ab

mak-ing fac-es and mak-ing friends like you. And when we grow up__ do you

think__ we'll see__ that I'm still like you__ and you're still__ like me?__

freely

I might be pret-ty, you might grow tall. But we don't have to change at

all.

rit. - - - - - -

Fine

Parents are People

BY CAROL HALL

Sisters and Brothers

MUSIC BY STEPHEN LAWRENCE
LYRICS BY BRUCE HART
ILLUSTRATED BY PETER REYNOLDS

Rock

1. Sis - ters and broth - ers,___
2. Broth-ers and sis - ters,___

broth-ers and sis - ters,___ Ain't we ev - 'ry___ one?___
sis - ters and broth - ers,___ Each and ev-'ry___ one.___

Broth-ers and sis - ters,___ sis - ters and broth - ers, ev-'ry fa - ther's daugh - ter, ev-'ry

Sis - ters and broth - ers,___ broth-ers and sis - ters, ev-'ry moth - er's daugh - ter, ev-'ry

moth-er's son.___

fa - ther's son.___

Helping

BY SHEL SILVERSTEIN

A-ga-tha Fry she made a pie, and Chris-toph-er John helped bake it.

Chris-toph-er John he mowed the lawn, and A-ga-tha Fry helped rake it.

Za-cha-ry Zugg took out the rug, and Jen-ni-fer Joy helped shake it.   And

Jen-ni-fer Joy she made a toy, and Za-cha-ry Zugg helped break it.___ And

some kind of help is the kind of help that help-ing's all a-bout. And

some kind of help is the kind of___ help we all can do with-out.

It's All Right to Cry

BY CAROL HALL

Moderate tempo

C (add D)

C (add D)   Dm7   G7   Dm7   G9sus4   C (add D)   C   C (add D)

It's all right to cry,   Cry-ing gets the sad out of you.   It's all right to
Rain-drops from your eyes,   Wash-ing all the mad out of you.   Rain-drops from your

Dm7   G7   Dm7   G   1. C   2. C   Am

cry,   It might make you feel bet-ter.
eyes,   It might make you feel   bet-ter.   It's all right to

William's Doll

MUSIC BY MARY RODGERS
LYRICS BY SHELDON HARNICK

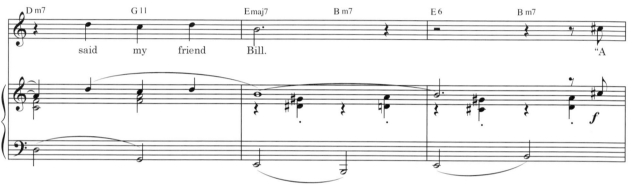

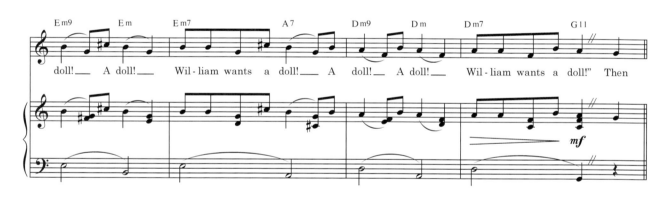

Bill said, "Base-ball's my fav-'rite game. I like to play but all the same, I'd give my

bat and ball___ and glove to have a doll that I___ could love." "How ver-y

doll!___ A doll! Wil - liam wants a doll!___ A doll!___ A doll!___ Wil - liam wants a doll!'" So

Wil - liam's grand - ma, as I've been told, bought Wil - liam a doll___ to hug and hold. And

Wil - liam's fa - ther be - gan to frown but grand - ma smiled and calmed him down, ex - plain - ing:

Faster

"Wil - liam wants a doll_____ so when he has a ba - by some -

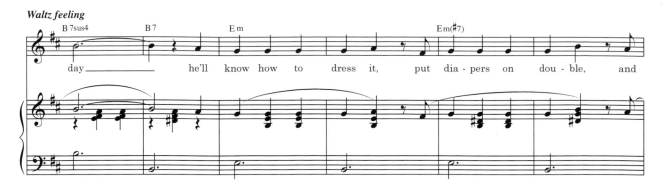

Waltz feeling

day _____ he'll know how to dress it, put dia - pers on dou - ble, and

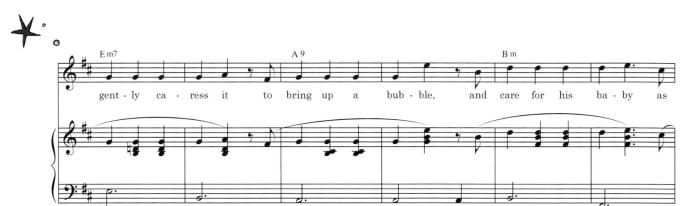

gent - ly ca - ress it to bring up a bub - ble, and care for his ba - by as

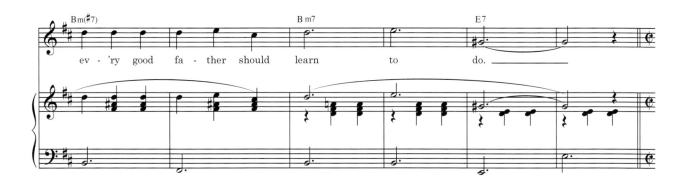

ev - 'ry good fa - ther should learn to do. _____

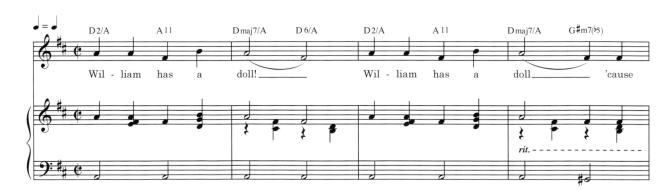

Wil - liam has a doll! _____ Wil - liam has a doll _____ 'cause

116

Free to Get Started

I 've often thought there ought to be a manual to hand to little kids, telling them what kind of planet they're on, why they don't fall off it, how much time they've probably got here, how to avoid poison ivy, and so on. I tried to write one once. It was called *Welcome to Earth*. But I got stuck on explaining why we don't fall off the planet. Gravity is just a word. It doesn't explain anything. If I could get past gravity, I'd tell them how we reproduce, how long we've been here, apparently, and a little bit about evolution. And one thing I would really like to tell them about is cultural relativity. I didn't learn until I was in college about all the other cultures, and I should have learned that in the first grade. A first grader should understand that his or her culture isn't a rational invention; that there are thousands of other cultures and they all work pretty well; that all cultures function on faith rather than truth; that there are lots of alternatives to our own society. Cultural relativity is defensible and attractive. It's also a source of hope. It means we don't have to continue this way if we don't like it.

—*Kurt Vonnegut, Jr.*

What Buying This Book will Do...

The book you hold in your hands has become a classic. That means children have loved it for many years—and maybe will always love it— for reasons you can see just by reading and looking.

Kids love to draw the pictures and listen to the magic rhymes even before they can read. Soon they understand the stories, laugh at the jokes, dress up like the characters, do plays at school or in their rooms, and sing the songs with their families in the car. The fun and togetherness only deepens when they grow up to share *Free To Be* with their own children.

Perhaps there is a country called Childhood where a part of each of us will always live. Parents who read this book re-visit that country. It's a place to learn about fairness and fun, daring and exploring, being sad or happy, and people who love you just as you are.

What has changed in the years since this book was born is the land around the country of Childhood.

I know a little girl who read *Free To Be* years ago, and learned it was okay to ask for equal space for girls in the playground. Now she is the mother of another little girl who is reading this book and learning it's okay to ask for equal space on television and in Congress. I know a little boy who read this book and saw that boys could have dolls. Now he is the father of another little boy who wants to save trees and animals and the planet.

No matter how much changes, Childhood will always be a place where we need to learn love and respect—for each other and for ourselves. That is the lesson you see in these pages.

But there is one important thing you can't see at all: how the money from buying this book is changing the world, too.

Its creators cared so much about the *Free To Be* message that they decided not to take the usual royalties from profits, but to use them to create the *Free To Be* Foundation.

Here are some of the things you can't see in these pages: Support for a clinic in a rural place where children didn't have doctors to go to; helping families in cities know that landlords can't discriminate against children; giving mothers good paying jobs in the mines by showing employers that childcare centers were possible; creating toys to make all children in childcare centers feel included; encouraging a special summer camp where girls learn to be strong; helping children in family day care get government support for good food; creating teaching materials that help to free children from sexual prejudices and fears; and supporting a national conference on helping boys grow up to be whole people.

The *Free To Be* Foundation will help the *Free To Be* message fly off the page and into real life.

—Gloria Steinem

The Rhyme & Reason
BEHIND "FREE TO BE... YOU AND ME"

In the minds of its creators—and of two generations of parents and teachers—the educational purpose of this book may have been inspiration, affirmation, and transformation. However to the millions of children who've been enthralled by *Free To Be . . . You and Me,* it's enough that it has delivered pure, unadulterated fun.

Now that you've reached its final pages, I hope that you, too, have relished Marlo's buoyant compendium of stories, songs, poems, art, and humor (whose last laugh is on old constraints and conventions).

But as an adult interloper, you may also have deduced that this happy hodge podge was conceived with care. The intention was to create children's stories that any grown-up could enjoy. To offer fantasy without false illusions, excitement without violence or cruelty, songs that you want to sing. To invent a new literature that, even as it delights and entertains, celebrates the wonder of human diversity and doesn't sideline any child because of race, gender, geography, household composition, religion, or family lifestyle.

You may have noticed life-enhancing messages woven into the merriment (though never at the cost of narrative grace or visual artistry). Some selections were designed to expand children's horizons and help them imagine a future without limits. Others were meant to dispel the stereotypes and myths that, unfortunately, even in the 21st century, continue to distort children's reality. (Like pretty-equals-good and boys-don't-cry.)

Several pieces challenged the societal expectations that stunt children's emotional expression or that restrict the types of kids, games, and toys that are considered "appropriate" for boys or girls to play with. Other pieces promoted friendship and cooperation, personal dignity and mutual respect, and a brotherhood that includes sisterhood.

I hope you will come back to this book often, and savor it as I did every time I shared it with my three children some 35 years ago and as I continue to do with my six grandchildren today. From this long experience, I can assure you that, with repeated exposure, *Free to Be*'s pleasures deepen and its meanings expand.

So snuggle up with your favorite small person, turn back to page one, and set off on the *Free To Be* adventure all over again. I promise you will never tire of this book.

—*Letty Cottin Pogrebin*
Editorial Consultant

Movers & Shakers

Marlo Thomas is an award-winning actress, author and activist whose varied body of work continues to have an impact on American entertainment and culture. She burst onto the scene in *That Girl*, the landmark TV series that broke new ground for young, independent woman, which she also conceived and produced. Her pioneering spirit continued with her creation of *Free to Be . . . You and Me*, which became a platinum album, a bestselling book, an Emmy Award-winning television special and a stage show. Marlo is the National Outreach Director for St. Jude Children's Research Hospital in Memphis, Tennessee, which was founded by her father, Danny Thomas, in 1962. She lives in New York with her husband, Phil Donahue.

Carole Hart (co-editor) is a multi- award-winning television and film producer/writer. She began her career in television working with her partner and husband, Bruce Hart, as one of the original writers of *Sesame Street* for which she received her first Emmy. After that she was asked by Marlo Thomas to help her manifest a vision of a project that would liberate children to feel free to be their authentic selves. That *was* the beginning of *Free To Be . . . You and Me*, and of a life-long collaboration and friendship. She was co-producer with Marlo of the *Free To Be* album and television special.

Elizabeth Law (contributing editor). Ms. Law is a children's book publisher who is passionate about turning children into life-long readers. She previously collaborated with Marlo Thomas on *Thanks and Giving All Year Long*

Christopher Cerf (contributing editor), has won five Emmy and two Grammy Awards for his writing, composing, and producing contributions to *Sesame Street*, *The Electric Company*, *Free to Be...A Family*, and the PBS series, *Between The Lions*,. He co-edited with Marlo, her book, *Thanks and Giving*.

Peter H. Reynolds is the founder of the media company and design studio FableVision, as well as the illustrator of many children's books, including *Someday* by Alison McGhee and the *Judy Moody* series by Megan McDonald.

Artists' Bios

Peter Sis, a winner of the MacArthur Genius Grant, is the author and illustrator of *Galileo* and multi-prize winning *The Wall*, his memoir of growing up in the Czech Republic.

Joe Mathieu has illustrated more than 100 books for children, including *Big Joe's Trailer Truck* and many books featuring the *Sesame Street*® Muppets.

Lynn Munsinger has illustrated many books by Helen Lester, including *Hurty Feelings*, and *What Grandmas Do Best* by Laura Numeroff.

Tony diTerlizzi's books include the Caldecott Honor *The Spider and the Fly*, *G is for One Gzonk*, and, with Holly Black, *The Spiderwick Chronicles*.

Henry Cole is the illustrator of the award-winning *And Tango Makes Three* by Peter Parnell and Justin Richardson, and *Little Bo* by Julie Andrews Edwards and Emma Walton Hamilton.

Jimmy Pickering is the illustrator of *Skelly the Skeleton Girl* and the *Araminta Spookie* books by Angie Sage.

David Catrow has collaborated on the *Silly Dilly* books with Alan Katz and illustrated *The Boy Who Wouldn't Share* by Mike Reiss, among many others.

LeUyen Pham's books for children include the bestseller *Big Sister, Little Sister* and the *Akimbo* series by Alexander McColl Smith.

Doug Taylor is a professional artist and illustrator whose work has appeared in *Sesame Street Magazine*.

Arnold Lobel, one of the great children's illustrators of the 20th century, created *Frog and Toad* and wrote and illustrated the Caldecott Award-winning book *Fables*.

127

Jerry Pinkney's many books for children include four Caldecott Honor Medal books, including *John Henry* and *The Ugly Duckling*.

Christopher Myers is the illustrator of *Jabberwocky*, a *New York Times* Best illustrated book, and *Jazz*, written by his father, Walter Dean Myers.

Dan Andreasen is the illustrator of *The Rose Year* series of Little House books, and many other books including *Pilot Pups* by Michelle Meadows.

Barbara Bascove's books for children include *The Green Hero: Early Adventures of Finn McCool* by Bernard Evslin.

Monica Sheehan is best-known for the lovable underdog character she creates for the back page of *Real Simple* magazine. She has illustrated more than twelve books, including *Be Happy*, *Prayers for All Occasions*, and *Be Green*.

Authors & Composers

Judy Blume ("The Pain and The Great One"). Ms. Blume has been writing books for children and adults for more than forty years. Her books include *Are You There God, It's Me Margaret*; *Tales of a Fourth Grade Nothing*; *Forever*; and the *Fudge* series.

Lucille Clifton ("Three Wishes"). A poet and children's writer, Ms. Clifton is the author of *Good Time*—a collection of poems—and the children's books *The Boy Who Didn't Believe in Spring*, *Some of the Days of Everett Anderson*, *The Black BC's*, and *Everett Anderson's Christmas Coming*. Today she is a Distinguished Professor of Humanities at St. Mary's College in Maryland.

Dan Greenburg ("Don't Dress Your Cat in an Apron" and "My Dog is a Plumber"). Mr. Greenburg has written numerous adult books in his career. He is also known for his two popular children's series *Maximum Boy* and *The Zach Files*, which was made into a television special.

Carol Hall ("Parents Are People," "It's All Right To Cry" and "Glad to Have a Friend Like You"). Ms. Hall's songs have been sung by Barbara Streisand, Neil Diamond, Shirley Bassey, Miriam Makeba, and Mabel Mercer. In addition, she has recorded two albums of her own material.

Sheldon Harnick (lyrics for "William's Doll"). Mr. Harnick has written the lyrics for many Broadway and off-Broadway revues and musicals, among them *Fiddler on the Roof*, *Fiorello*, *The Apple Tree*, and *The Rothschilds*. In addition to his numerous awards, including Tony and Grammy Awards, and a Pulitzer Prize for Drama, he also wrote songs for HBO's version of *The Tale of Peter Rabbit* starring Carol Burnett.

Bruce Hart (lyrics for "Free to Be . . . You and Me" and "Sisters and Brothers"). Mr. Hart won an Emmy Award as one of the original writers of *Sesame Street*. He also wrote the lyrics for its title song. With Stephen Lawrence, he co-produced the musical portions of the record *Free to Be . . . You and Me*. He also co-wrote the script, wrote the lyrics for, and directed the NBC musical movie, *Sooner or Later*, as well as the best-selling young adult book, *Sooner or Later*, and its sequels.

Joyce (Glassman) Johnson ("The Old Woman Who Lived in a Shoe"). Ms. Johnson has written both fiction and nonfiction books and articles for *Harper's Bazaar*, *The New Yorker*, and *Vanity Fair*. In 1987, she won the National Book Critics Circle Award for her book *Minor Characters*, her memoir about New York City during the 1950's Beat Generation.

Elaine Laron ("What are Little Boys Made Of?", "No One Else" and "The Sun and the Moon"). As Writer and Head Lyricist for educational TV's series *The Electric Company*, Ms. Laron wrote the lyrics of more than thirty of its songs. She has also written and produced several anti-war records, including *Hell, No, I Ain't Gonna Go!*

Stephen Lawrence (music for "Free To Be . . . You and Me," "When We Grow Up," and "Sisters and Brothers"). Mr. Lawrence's more than 250 songs have been recorded by Petula Clark, Cass Elliot, Helen Reddy, Diana Ross, The New Seekers, and others. With Bruce Hart, he co-produced the musical portions of the record *Free To Be…You and Me*. He has won three Emmy Awards for his work on *Sesame Street* and arranged the music for this book.

Betty Miles ("Atalanta"). Ms. Miles has written more than thirty children's books, including *Hey I'm Reading!,* the first book for children and their families who are learning to read. She served as editor for the *Bank Street* series of books.

Shelley Miller ("When We Grow Up"). An English major who turned to singing and song-writing, Ms. Miller has worked with Stephen Lawrence for several years.

Carl Reiner (co-author "Boy Meets Girl"). Mr. Reiner has gained fame as an actor, writer, director, producer, and recording star. He won two Emmy awards for his work on the *Sid Caesar* shows and six as producer and writer for the *Dick Van Dyke* series. He has written nine books, including the children's picture book, *Tell Me a Scary Story but Not Too Scary.*

Phil Ressner ("Dudley Pippin and the Principal"). In addition to his book of *Dudley Pippin* stories, from which the selection in this book is adapted, Mr. Ressner wrote the children's books *August Explains, Jerome, At Night,* and *The Park in the City.*

Mary Rodgers (music for "William's Doll" and adaptation of "Ladies First"). A composer and writer, Ms. Rodgers composed the score for the Broadway musical *Once Upon a Mattress.* Her children's books include *The Rotten Book, Freaky Friday, A Billion for Boris,* and *Summer Switch.* For several years she served as chairwoman of the Julliard School's trustees.

Anne Roiphe ("The Field"). Ms. Roiphe is the author of both fiction and nonfiction works. Her second novel, *Up the Sandbox,* was a best-seller and was made into a feature film, starring Barbara Streisand. Her work of nonfiction, *Fruitful: A Memoir of Modern Motherhood,* was a finalist for the 1996 National Book Award.

David Slavin ("If Wishes Were Fishes"). Mr. Slavin's cultural and political satire has been featured in *The New York Times, The Los Angeles Times,* Salon.com, and on *National Public Radio*'s "All Things Considered."

Shel Silverstein ("Helping" and "Ladies First"). Mr. Silverstein was an artist, cartoonist, writer, jazz singer, and composer. He wrote the song "A Boy Named Sue" for Johnny Cash and in 1998 he collaborated with his friends Waylon Jennings, Mel Tillis, Bobby Bare, and Jerry Reed on the album *Old Dogs.* His books for children include *The Giving Tree, A Light in the Attic, Where the Sidewalk Ends,* and his last published work *Falling Up.*

Linda Sitea ("Zachary's Divorce"). An artist and writer, Ms. Sitea studied in California and New York. "Zachary's Divorce" is her first published story.

Peter Stone (co-author "Boy Meets Girl"). Mr. Stone won a Tony Award and New York Drama Critics Award for *1776,* and three additional Tony Awards for Best Book of a Musical for *Woman of the Year, Titanic,* and *Curtains.* H also won an Academy Award for *Father Goose,* an Emmy Award for *The Defenders,* and the Mystery Writers of America Award for the movie *Charade.*

Judith Viorst ("The Southpaw"). Ms. Viorst has published many books including the adult books *Suddenly Sixty and Other Shocks of Later Life* and *I'm Too Young to Be Seventy: And Other Delusions.* She is probably best known for her popular *Alexander* series, including *Alexander and the Terrible, Horrible, No Good, Very Bad Day.*

Charlotte Zolotow (The book *William's Doll,* from which the selection in this book is adapted). Ms. Zolotow is the author of more than seventy children's books, including *The Seashore Book, The Moon Was the Best,* and *Mr. Rabbit and the Lovely Present.* She was an editor at Harper Junior Books for more than thirty-eight years, and in 1998 The Charlotte Zolotow Award was established in her name to honor the best picture book manuscripts published in the United States.

Free to Be a Doodler,
an Artist, a Poet, a Writer, a Dreamer
(THESE ARE YOUR PAGES!)